The HEN HOUSE
AND DOG HOUSE TOO

VIKING/PUFFIN
Published by the Penguin Group: London, New York, Australia, Canada and New Zealand
Penguin Books Ltd, Registered Offices: Harmondsworth, Middlesex, England

First published by Viking 1999
1 3 5 7 9 10 8 6 4 2
Published in Puffin Books 1999
1 3 5 7 9 10 8 6 4 2

Text copyright © Allan Ahlberg, 1999
Illustrations copyright © André Amstutz, 1999

Printed in Hong Kong by Imago Publishing Ltd

A CIP catalogue record for this book is available from the British Library
ISBN 0–670–87993–2 Hardback
ISBN 0–140–56399–7 Paperback

It is bedtime in the Hen House.
Mother Hen is bathing the chickens.
Slow Dog is watching TV.
Tiptoe, tiptoe!
And *somebody* is creeping up.

It is bedtime in the Hen House.
Mother Hen is telling a story
to the chickens.
Slow Dog is making a sandwich.
Tiptoe, tiptoe!
And *somebody* is creeping in.

It is bedtime in the Hen House.
Mother Hen is kissing
the chickens goodnight.
Slow Dog is dozing in his chair.
Tiptoe, tiptoe!
And *somebody* is hiding.

Time goes by.
The moon comes up.
The clock strikes ten.

Mother Hen is fast asleep.
The chickens are fast asleep.
Slow Dog is fast asleep.
Somebody . . .

. . . is wide awake.

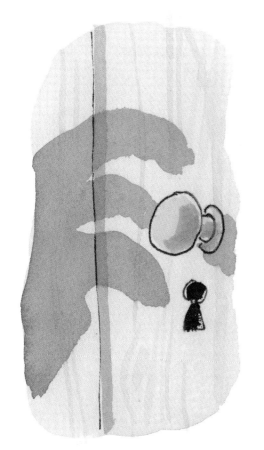

Tiptoe, tiptoe!
Somebody is on the stairs.
Tiptoe, tiptoe!
Somebody is at the door.

Tiptoe, tiptoe!
Somebody is by the bed.

Somebody is *counting the chickens.*
One chicken –
yes!
Two chickens –
yes, yes!
Three chickens –
yes, yes, yes!

Slow Dog sits up in bed.

Slow Dog
puts on his slippers.

Slow Dog
goes . . . sleepwalking.

Cheep, cheep! Cheep, cheep!
The chickens are in trouble.
Cheep, cheep! Cheep, cheep!
The chickens are in a sack.
Cheep, cheep! Cheep, cheep!
Somebody has *got* them.

Slow Dog sleepwalks
from his room.
Slow Dog sleepwalks
on the landing.

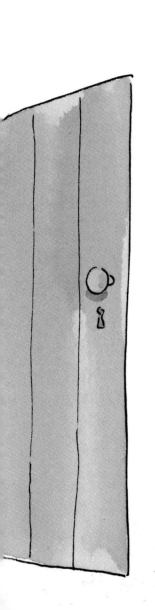

Slow Dog sleepwalks out of the window.

Slow Dog . . . .

falls.

Oh no!
Poor Slow Dog!
Is he hurt?
No, Slow Dog is not hurt.
But *somebody* is.

Mother Hen wakes up.

She runs outside
to find her chickens.

One chicken – yes!

Two chickens – yes, yes!

Three chickens –
yes, yes, yes!

It is midnight in
the Hen House.
The chickens are
back in bed.

Slow Dog
is back in bed.
Tiptoe, tiptoe!
And *somebody*
is limping home.

The End

The HEN HOUSE

AND NOW TURN OVER

THE FAST FOX, SLOW DOG BOOKS

If you liked this story,
why not read another?
Try

Chicken, Chips and Peas

In *Chicken, Chips and Peas,*
Fast Fox is hungry. He wants his supper.
Chips – yes!
Peas – yes!
And chicken –
YES!

Oh no! Those poor little chickens . . .

. . . who will save them?